Cat's Colors

for Julian &
Jerry~lee

a BIG
thank you
to Genevieve

Cat's Colors

*Jane Cabrera

PUFFIN BOOKS

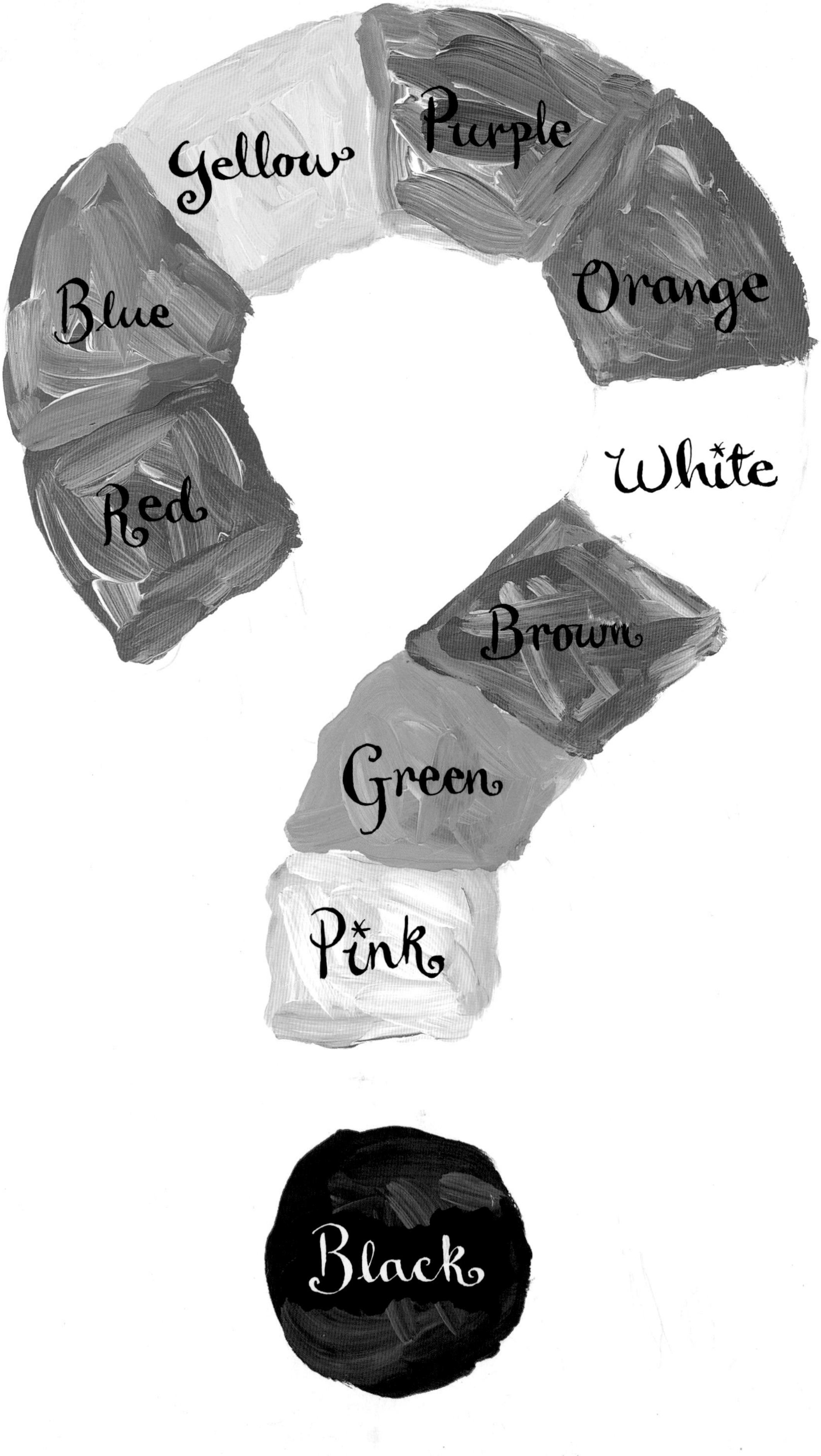

Gellow

Purple

Blue

Orange

Red

White

Brown

Green

Pink

Black

Is it Green? Green is the grass where I like to walk.

Is it **Pink**?

Pink are the petals
of my favorite
flowers.

Is it
Black?
Black is the night
when bats
swoop and soar.

Is it Red?.
Red is the rug
where I snooze
by the fire.

Is it **Yellow?**
Yellow is
the sand
on the
sunny
beach.

Is it Brown?
Brown is the earth
where I dig my holes.

Is it Blue?
Blue is the sky where
I chase the birds.

Is it **White**?

White are the clouds floating in the sky.

Is it Orange?

Yes! because...

Orange is the color of my mother.

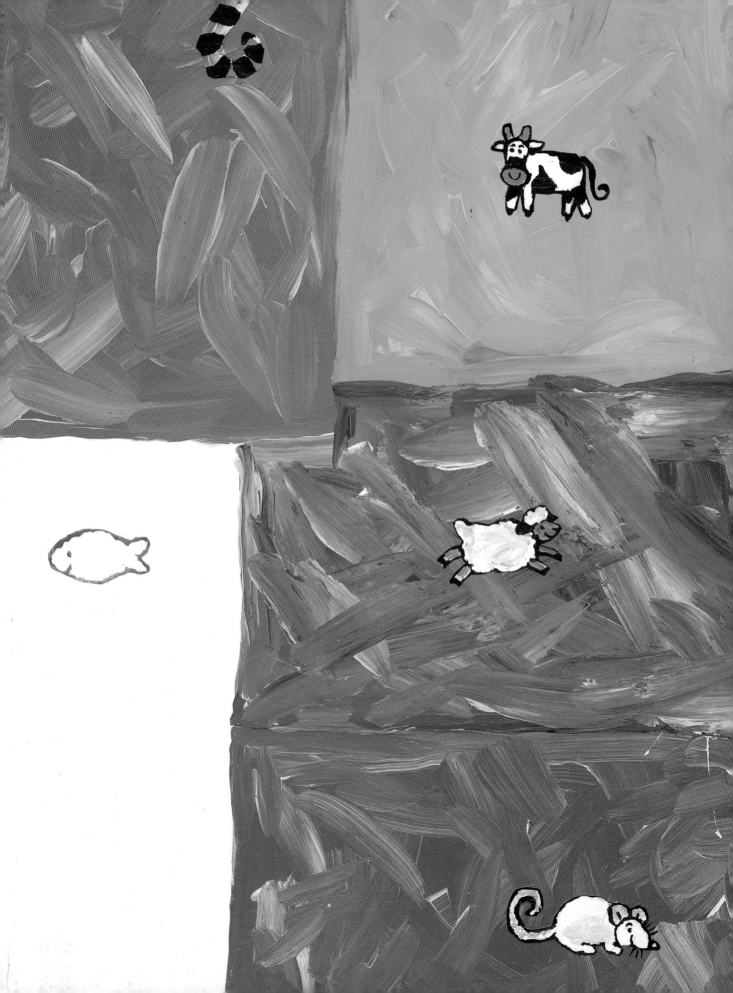

PUFFIN BOOKS
Published by the Penguin Group
Penguin Putnam Books for Young Readers,
345 Hudson Street, New York, New York 10014, U.S.A.
Penguin Books Ltd, 27 Wrights Lane, London W8 5TZ, England
Penguin Books Australia Ltd, Ringwood, Victoria, Australia
Penguin Books Canada Ltd, 10 Alcorn Avenue, Toronto, Ontario, Canada M4V 3B2
Penguin Books (N.Z.) Ltd, 182-190 Wairau Road, Auckland 10, New Zealand

Penguin Books Ltd, Registered Offices: Harmondsworth, Middlesex, England

Published in Great Britain by Reed Children's Books as *Cat's Colours*, 1997
First published in the United States of America by Dial Books For Young Readers,
a division of Penguin Putnam Books for Young Readers, 1997
Published by Puffin Books, a member of Penguin Putnam Books for Young Readers, 2000

5 7 9 10 8 6 4

Copyright © Jane Cabrera, 1997

THE LIBRARY OF CONGRESS HAS CATALOGED THE DIAL EDITION AS FOLLOWS:
Cabrera, Jane.
Cat's colors / Jane Cabrera.—1st ed. p. cm.
Simultaneously published in Great Britain.
Summary: A cat describes ten different colors and tells which one is its favorite.
ISBN 0-8037-2090-4 (tr.) [1. Color—Fiction. 2. Cats—Fiction.] I. Title.
PZ7.C1135Cat 1997 [E]—dc20 96-11765 CIP AC

Puffin Books ISBN 0-14-056487-X

Printed in Dubai

3 1333 03561 4906